The Lost Puppy

The Lost Puppy

Holly Webb

Illustrated by Sophy Williams

Stripes

For Max, and for Georgie Dog

For more information about Holly Webb visit:
www.holly-webb.com

STRIPES PUBLISHING
An imprint of Magi Publications
1 The Coda Centre, 189 Munster Road,
London SW6 6AW

A paperback original
First published in Great Britain in 2012

Text copyright © Holly Webb, 2012
Illustrations copyright © Sophy Williams, 2012

ISBN: 978-1-84715-224-4

A CIP catalogue record for this book is available
from the British Library.

Printed and bound in the UK.

10 9 8 7 6 5 4 3 2 1

Chapter One

"Ruby! Happy Birthday!" Auntie Nell rushed down the garden path to hug Ruby, with Maisie the dachshund galloping after her.

"Hey, Maisie, where are the puppies?" Ruby asked. Ever since Maisie had her puppies, she'd been curled up in her pen in the kitchen with them, as though she didn't dare let them out of her sight.

Auntie Nell shook her head. "I think she's getting a bit fed up with them now they're so much bigger. They spend all their time climbing over her, and nipping each other's ears, or Maisie's. They can't get over the board we've got across the kitchen door, but their mum can, and she's left them behind to have a bit of a break."

"Can we go and see them?" Ruby asked. She'd always loved playing with Maisie, but the puppies were even more gorgeous than their mum, and she hadn't seen them for a week. She was sure they'd have changed. They were eleven weeks old now, but they still seemed to be growing so fast she could almost see it happening.

"Puppies!" her three-year-old sister Anya demanded, stomping up the garden path. She loved the puppies as much as Ruby did. Ruby actually wondered if sometimes Anya thought she *was* a puppy. She curled up in their basket almost every time they came to visit Auntie Nell. Once she'd even tried their puppy food, but luckily she hadn't liked it.

"And hello to you too, Anya." Auntie Nell grinned, as Anya hurried past her into the house. Ruby chased after her little sister – if she wasn't quick she'd probably find Anya sitting in the water bowl.

"So are you having a good birthday?" Auntie Nell asked. "Does it feel odd that you've already had your party?" Ruby had shared her birthday party with her best friend Beth the previous weekend. Beth was two weeks older than Ruby, so they'd split the difference.

"No, it's great!" Ruby beamed at her. "It feels like I'm having two birthdays!"

"Well, I've got a present for you, in the house." Auntie Nell was looking a bit smug and secretive, Ruby realized. She started to feel excited about the present. She looked round at her mum and dad, wondering if they knew what it was. Mum had exactly the same expression on her face as Auntie Nell, which Ruby supposed wasn't that strange, as they were sisters.

"What is it?" she asked curiously.

"Why don't you come and see the puppies before you open your present?" Auntie Nell suggested. "Otherwise we'll find them all nibbling Anya's toes. It's nearly their lunchtime."

The puppies were still having lots of small meals. "Is it porridge?" Ruby asked hopefully, as they went through to the kitchen. The last time they'd visited, the puppies had eaten milky porridge, and all of them had dangled their big ears in the bowl – and came out with porridge-crusted ears afterwards. It was really funny!

Auntie Nell laughed. "No, sorry, it's just biscuits. Very boring. But they like them. Now they're old enough for their new homes, I'm weaning them off the milky stuff."

"Are they really big enough to leave Maisie?" Ruby asked, peering round the kitchen door at the seething mass of brown and black puppies wriggling around in their pen. Maisie hopped elegantly over the board in the doorway, and headed back to her babies. The puppies saw her coming and flung themselves out of the pen, then scampered across the floor to their mum. Ruby giggled. She was sure that she saw Maisie duck her head and dig her paws in as she was hit by a wave of puppies.

Auntie Nell nodded. "A couple of people have come to see them already."

"Six babies," Ruby murmured to Dad, as she crouched down to get closer to the pups. "You always say me and Anya are enough!"

Dad nodded. "Quite enough!"

"I think she'll miss them when they're gone," Auntie Nell said. "But right now I don't think she's going to mind *that* much. And I am keeping one puppy."

"Oh, which one?" Ruby asked, crossing her fingers behind her back.

"The little black girl puppy. I'm calling her Millie. She gets on well with Maisie, I think. And I like the names both beginning with 'M'."

Ruby nodded, a little sadly. She had been hoping that Auntie Nell would keep her favourite puppy, the gorgeous boy with the black back and russety-orange paws. He'd spotted her coming in, and now he trotted over to her eagerly. In her head, she'd named him Toby, although she hadn't told anyone.

There was no point naming him really, as he would be going off to live somewhere else, horribly soon. But Ruby hadn't been able to help it. Toby was just the perfect name for him.

He was such a funny little dog, always bouncing about. Ruby rolled a jingly ball across the kitchen floor for him, and he skidded after it eagerly, his paws slipping around on the tiles. He was dashing after it so fast that he overshot, and had to screech to a halt and snatch it out of Millie's paws. His sister growled at him crossly, and stomped away.

Toby picked up the ball in his sharp little teeth, and marched triumphantly back to Ruby, his ears swinging jauntily. Then he dropped it at her feet, wagging his tail and nosing it towards her, asking her to do it again.

Ruby stroked his glossy fur. "Oh, you're so gorgeous."

Anya, who had been lying on the kitchen floor so as to be on the same level with the puppies, wriggled her way over to Ruby and Toby, and nuzzled him, nose to nose. Toby looked slightly shocked, but he nuzzled her too, and then licked her generously all down one cheek.

Anya squealed with delight, and was about to lick him back when Mum grabbed her. "No licking the puppies!"

Mum glanced worriedly at Dad, but he was laughing.

"It'll be fine," he told her.

Ruby frowned at them. What did

they mean? She was sure Toby licking Anya just once wouldn't do her any harm.

"Why don't you pick him up?" Auntie Nell asked her. "He won't mind."

Ruby gently slipped her hands under Toby's smooth tummy, and snuggled him against her. He had climbed into her lap before, but she had never actually picked him up properly. He was so good to cuddle. She sighed quietly as she rubbed her cheek against his warm head, wondering if this was the last time she would see him.

Toby sighed too, but happily. He dug his nose under the shoulder of Ruby's jumper, which made her giggle and squirm, then he scrabbled his claws against the fabric lovingly.

Auntie Nell smiled at her. "So, do you like your present?"

Ruby looked up, confused.

Dad laughed, and Mum smiled at her, then eyed Toby meaningfully.

"Toby? The puppy, I mean?" Ruby stared at them all, her mouth falling open in surprise.

"I told you she'd already named him!" Auntie Nell said. "He's always been the one Ruby liked best. A lady wanted to choose him yesterday, Ruby, but I told her he was reserved for you!"

"You're giving me Toby for my

birthday?" Ruby sounded dazed. "Can we take him home?" she added hopefully. "Or is he mine but at your house?" Mum and Dad had always said no to a dog before, because Anya was too young. She looked up at them uncertainly. "You said not while Anya was little…"

"But he's not going to get big enough to knock Anya over, is he?" Dad pointed out. Toby was a miniature dachshund – he'd never be bigger than about thirty centimetres tall. "And yes, he's coming home with us. Mum and I have decided you're both old enough now. He'll be yours mostly, Ruby, but Anya's allowed to cuddle him too, OK?"

Ruby nodded. She didn't mind sharing at all. She was still gobsmacked that they were actually getting their own dog! "Are we taking him home *today*?" she asked Auntie Nell.

"Absolutely. But you have to eat lunch first. And I made you another birthday cake!"

"Oh wow! Oh, I have to call Beth and tell her we're really getting a dog," Ruby whispered. But then she looked worried. "Don't we need stuff? A basket … and bowls … and … loads of things…"

Auntie Nell held up one finger. "Just a moment." She disappeared into the utility room, and came back out with a huge cardboard box. "One perfect puppy parcel. This is your present from me, Ruby. Toby is from your mum and dad, so I said I would give you all the things you'd need to look after him properly." She dumped the box down in front of Ruby. "It's heavy!"

Toby wriggled in Ruby's arms, curious to see what was in such a huge box. Ruby laughed. "I think you and Anya are going to be fighting over it," she told him. "Anya loves boxes." She hugged Toby gently. It was still hard to believe he was really hers!

Chapter Two

Toby travelled the twenty-minute journey to Ruby's house in a special cardboard box with flaps and a handle on top, which Auntie Nell had given them. But Mum had said that Ruby could get him out as soon as the car pulled up at the house.

When Ruby opened the flaps, Toby was squashed into the corner of the box

with his special blar.
looking very worried.
understand what was h.
he didn't like all the lur.
The box smelled strange ı , sort of
new and biscuity. He was glad he had
the blanket, which smelled of home,
and the other puppies, and his mum.
But he dropped it when he saw Ruby
and wagged his tail, just a little. He
didn't stir out of his corner though.

"Hey, Toby…" Ruby whispered. "Are
you OK? Was it scary being in the car?"

Toby edged closer to her and stood
with his front paws on the side of the
box, looking up at her hopefully.
He didn't like it in here. He wanted to
be stroked and fussed over. And fed.
He was starving.

Ruby laughed as she picked him up and he nibbled at her jacket. "Are you hungry? Auntie Nell didn't want to feed you before we drove home – she said you might be sick. And she thought it would be good to feed you here, you see. Then you'll have good first memories of being with us. In your new home!"

Toby barked – a sharp, demanding, "Feed me!" bark. He was sure he knew what Ruby was talking about. Auntie Nell always talked to the puppies. *Shall we feed you now, hmm?* That was what she said when she was getting the yummy biscuits out.

"Come on then!" Ruby followed Mum inside, and Dad staggered after them with the huge box, while Anya danced around them, singing a little dog-song she'd made up.

"We've got to do a bit of unpacking and then you'll get your dinner," Ruby explained to Toby, as she put him down gently on the kitchen floor. "Your bowls are in here, and a big bag of the food you like."

But Toby was distracted from food for a moment, as he looked around the kitchen. Dad quickly closed the door. "We've got to keep him in here for a few days, remember," he told Ruby. "Auntie Nell said to get him used to one room first."

"And it's tiles in here," Mum added. "So we can wipe up if he makes any puddles. I know Auntie Nell's started house-training him, but he's bound to be a bit confused, and he might forget he has to go out to wee. We'd better put some newspaper down too, just in case."

Ruby carefully unpacked the box, admiring the cute bowls Auntie Nell had got, with little bones painted on them, and the soft red padded basket.

"Look! There's a collar and lead!"

"Oh yes. We'll have to get a tag with our phone number put on that." Dad nodded. "Here's the food, shall I open it, Ruby? Then you can give him some."

Ruby carefully used the measuring cup to fill the bowl with food – Auntie Nell had explained about measuring out the right amount of puppy biscuits for Toby's size.. As she put it down, Toby immediately stopped sniffing his way along the kitchen units, and raced for the food bowl like some sort of trained sniffer dog. He gulped down the biscuits in huge mouthfuls, licking all the way round the bowl in case he'd missed some. Then he had a long drink of water.

"His tummy's nearly touching the ground!" Ruby pointed out. It was true. Toby's little dachshund legs meant he wasn't that high off the ground anyway, and now his stomach looked like a small balloon underneath him. He gave a huge yawn, licked round his mouth again, and then looked around for somewhere to collapse and sleep off his enormous tea. He stomped over to his basket, where Ruby had put the special blanket Auntie Nell had given them. She'd explained that it had been in the pen with Maisie and the puppies for the last few days, so that Toby would have something that smelled familiar.

"Oh, Anya!" Mum sighed.

Toby's new bed was already occupied. Anya was curled up in the soft basket, fast asleep. Toby looked at her doubtfully, and then turned to look up at Ruby, with his ears hitched up just a little in a, *Well, what am*

I supposed to do about this, then? sort of way.

Mum gently lifted Anya out of the basket, but Toby clearly wasn't sure about it now. He stood at Ruby's feet, staring up at her pleadingly, and she knelt down next to him. Toby gave a little sigh of relief and heaved himself on to her lap, scrabbling round her knees a couple of times, and then slumping down in a heap – fast asleep.

Toby settled into his new home very quickly. And he was growing up, too. He was still small – he was never going to be a big dog – but over the next couple of weeks he stopped sleeping so much, and became more and more adventurous – and a bit naughty. He loved playing in the garden with Ruby and Anya, especially rootling through the flowerbeds. Then he would trot happily back to the girls, covered in leaves and bits of twig, and shake himself all over them.

He was also terribly nosy. As soon as he was allowed out of the kitchen, after the first couple of days, he investigated the entire house. Every time Ruby wasn't watching he would manage to find himself another secret hiding place, which he would get stuck in. Then he'd howl so she had to come and rescue him. Ruby didn't understand how he actually managed to find half the spots, let alone climb into them. When he got trapped behind the washing machine Dad had to pull it right out from the wall for Toby to escape.

For a dog with such short legs, he was a very good climber, although he was much better at climbing up than down. That never stopped him, though.

About a week after they'd got Toby, Ruby let him out into the garden on his own for the first time. Up until now she'd always gone with him, but he needed a wee, and she was helping Mum do some cooking.

Ruby had just set the oven timer for the chocolate chip cookies they were baking, when she realized he was still outside. She looked out of the kitchen window, but she couldn't see him.

"Maybe he's sitting by the door, waiting to come in," Mum suggested.

But he wasn't. Feeling worried, Ruby ran outside, hoping that Toby hadn't found a gap under the fence. She and Dad had gone all the way round the garden checking it for holes when they'd first brought him home, but what if they'd missed one?

She raced down the garden, calling anxiously. "Toby! Toby!"

Mum stood on the patio, carrying

Anya, and peered into the flowerbeds.

Suddenly, Anya laughed and pointed, and Ruby heard a worried little whine somewhere up above her.

"Toby! How did you get up there?"

He was standing in the doorway of Ruby's treehouse, staring down uncertainly. The treehouse had been Ruby's birthday present the year before, and it had clever steps built round the tree trunk. Obviously Toby had managed to scramble up, but he wasn't so sure about getting down again.

"Oh, Toby! You aren't supposed to go climbing!" Dachshunds' long backs meant stairs weren't good for them – Ruby was amazed that he had even managed to get up the steps. She reached for Toby, and he wriggled into her arms gratefully so she could carry him down. Then he ran all around the garden twice, as though he liked the feel of solid ground under his paws.

Getting stuck in the treehouse didn't teach Toby to be any more cautious, as Ruby had hoped it might. He was still only a very little dog, but he seemed to think he was enormous, and he had no fear at all.

A few weeks after they had brought him home, once he had had all his vaccinations and been microchipped, Toby was ready to go out for his first walk.

Ruby fetched his beautiful blue lead. They were taking Toby to the park – and she knew he would love it!

"Toby, keep still!" She was trying to clip the lead on to his collar, but Toby kept wriggling. He'd never worn the lead before, but somehow he knew it meant something exciting.

"Let me check your collar too…" Ruby whispered. Auntie Nell had told her that it was important to fit his collar properly – not so loose it would slip off, but not so tight it would rub. She was supposed to be able to put her finger between Toby's neck and the collar. "I'll open it up one more hole, it's a bit tight on you. Toby, stop jumping!" She giggled as he wriggled again and licked her nose.

Ruby was a bit worried that Toby would be nervous as they walked to the park – especially with the noisy cars speeding past. But he bounced along happily, sniffing everything they passed. His claws clicked busily on the pavement as he scurried from side to side, occasionally darting behind Ruby as he caught another interesting whiff. Ruby kept having to stop and unwind the lead from around her ankles.

"Are you all right, Ruby? Do you want me to take him?" Dad asked. Mum was walking with Anya, who was just as much trouble as Toby, and didn't have a lead, unfortunately.

"No." Ruby shook her head firmly. Toby was her special responsibility, and she had to be able to look after him. Surely it couldn't be *that* difficult to go for a walk?

At last they reached the park. It wasn't very far away, but Toby had probably covered three times the distance by going forwards, backwards and sideways, and he was looking a bit weary. But as soon as he saw the huge expanse of green grass, and the other dogs racing around, he brightened up immediately, his tail starting to whip from side to side. He sniffed busily at several clumps of grass, and then followed Ruby along one of the paths.

"Shall we see what he thinks of the ducks?" Dad suggested.

"Knowing Toby, he'll think that they were put there for him to play with," Mum sighed. But they headed through the park towards the ducks, with Anya running ahead – the ducks were her favourite thing.

"Oh, watch out, Anya!" Mum called, seeing a man coming down the path with a big German shepherd dog. Anya loved dogs, and she wanted to stroke all of them – even if they looked big, and possibly a bit fierce, like this one.

Toby spotted the German shepherd at the same moment as Anya did, and he darted forward, dragging his lead out of Ruby's hand.

"Toby!" Ruby squeaked in horror, watching him galloping away. She looked down at her hand, as though she was still expecting the lead to be in it. Then she raced after him.

Toby ran up to the huge German shepherd, and barked loud, shrill barks at it. He could see Anya next to the bigger dog. She was his, even if she did keep sleeping in his basket. He wasn't going to let some big strange dog scare her. He danced around the huge dog – barking and yapping until he ran out of breath and had to sit down, panting.

The poor German shepherd hadn't even thought of hurting Anya, and was too well-trained to do anything to Toby either. She took a confused step backwards, towards her owner. She was worried she might be in trouble, and it was all very unfair.

But her owner patted her. "Good girl, Tara. Sit, there's a good girl." The man then reached down and picked up Toby in one hand – while Toby wriggled and yapped and fought.

Ruby came running up. Mum and Dad were chasing after them, too.

"Here you go." The man handed the wriggling puppy to Ruby.

"I'm really sorry! It's his first walk – he doesn't really understand other dogs yet..." Ruby stammered, hoping the German shepherd's owner wasn't going to shout at her.

"Sorry!" Dad gasped, as he caught Anya up. "I hope he didn't upset your dog."

Toby was still yapping at the German shepherd, who was now

sitting beautifully and looking rather smug, as though she knew she was well-behaved and the little yappy dog wasn't.

"Just be careful. Not all dogs are as calm as Tara," her owner told Ruby kindly, and he nodded at Dad.

"I won't let him run off again," Ruby promised.

"I'm so sorry about that!" Dad said, holding tight to Anya, who was reaching out hopefully as the big dog paced past. "No, Anya, you can't stroke her. We shouldn't have let you get so close."

"Let's get home before we get into any more trouble," Mum said, looking around anxiously at all the other dogs in the park.

As the German shepherd and her owner headed off down the path, Ruby hugged Toby tight. He was still staring suspiciously after the bigger dog, his little body tense with anxiety as he pulled in her arms.

"Oh, Toby!" she whispered. "That dog could have eaten a puppy like you for breakfast!"

"And had room for a couple more," Dad added grimly.

Chapter Three

"It was so embarrassing," Ruby said, blushing as she remembered the disastrous walk the day before. "And then on the way back home there was another big dog – a Labrador – and Toby barked at him, too!"

Ruby had hurried into school that morning to talk to Beth before they went into class. Beth had known they were taking Toby for his first walk that weekend – Ruby had been so excited about it on Friday.

Beth nodded. "I wonder if it's a small dog thing? My gran's got a Westie called Billy, and he barks at *everything*. Gran says it's because he knows he's little and he feels like he's got a lot to prove. Toby might grow out of it," she suggested, a bit doubtfully.

Ruby sighed. "Maybe. He's so sweet most of the time – you know he is. But I just couldn't get him to stop barking! Mum rang Auntie Nell, and she says we might need to take him to obedience classes. Mum called and signed him up for some, but they don't start for a few weeks. I don't know what we're going to do until then!"

"I'm sure puppy training will help. He isn't really bad-tempered. Just yappy. He's a gorgeous dog, Ruby." Beth smiled, remembering. When she'd come over to tea last week, Toby had curled up on her lap and fallen asleep. When it was time for Beth to go home, Ruby had had to pick him up off her lap still asleep and all saggy, like a Beanie Baby dog.

"Maybe he just needs to get used to other dogs," Ruby said. "Or perhaps you're right, and he will grow out of it. But I need to make sure I hold on to him really tightly until he does."

Beth frowned thoughtfully. "Couldn't you take him somewhere quieter for walks for now?" she suggested. "Somewhere with not as many dogs, I mean."

Ruby nodded. "That's a good idea. I'll ask Mum and Dad if they can think of anywhere. It's half-term next week, so we should have a bit more time for walks." She hugged Beth quickly, as the bell rang. "You're a star!"

Ruby's mum was pleased with the idea of a quiet walk. She thought that it would be a fun way to start the half-term holiday, after school on Friday afternoon.

"What about those woods we go past on the way to your dance class? Norbury Copse?" she suggested. "People do take their dogs there, but I wouldn't have thought many people would be out in the middle of a Friday afternoon."

"That would be great!" Ruby agreed.

When they got out of school on Friday, she said goodbye to Beth – who was going to stay at her gran's for the week – and rushed to the car, flinging her PE bag into the boot.

Toby was sitting in his new wire travel crate, looking worried. He still wasn't sure about going in the car, and he wasn't really keen on being shut in the crate, but at least he had more space than in the old cardboard carrier.

The woods were only about quarter of an hour's drive away, and soon Ruby was lifting Toby out, letting him sniff busily around the grassy verge they had parked beside. There were only a couple of other cars there – it looked like the woods would be good and empty.

It was a gorgeous autumn day, really warm for October, and Toby had a brilliant time racing along with Ruby, and flinging himself into piles of dry leaves. They flew everywhere as he rolled and jumped and snapped at them, growling as though he were very fierce. His legs were so short that every so often he disappeared right into a drift of leaves, and then he would come up spluttering and do it all over again.

Ruby was laughing so much her tummy hurt. The way Toby's ears flapped when he jumped made him look as though he was trying to take off!

"Oooh, river!" Anya called excitedly, as they came to a little stream running along between deep, sloping banks.

There was an old rickety-looking wooden bridge, and they stood on it throwing sticks in and watching them float past underneath the bridge. Toby watched them in bewilderment, unsure why anyone would waste good sticks dropping them in the water. He whined and tugged on the lead, wanting to go and explore some more, and at last they went over the bridge and deeper into the woods.

Ruby and Toby were chasing Anya through the leaves, when suddenly Toby stopped, staring off down the little winding path they were following. He'd heard something, Ruby could tell. He looked as though he was listening with every hair of his body. Then she heard it too – barking, but much further into the woods. They weren't going to have the place to themselves after all.

"Oh, is it another dog?" Mum said, with a sigh. "Hold tight to him, Ruby. Or I can take him, if you like?"

"It's OK." Ruby wound the lead round her hand, as Toby let off a series of earsplitting barks. He jumped around at the end of his lead, wanting to chase after the other dog, but Ruby wouldn't let go.

Anya stared at Toby, wide-eyed. She didn't like it when Toby barked loudly. She backed away, meaning to grab hold of Mum's hand, but she wasn't looking where she was going. She tripped over a tree root and fell, scraping the side of her face against the rocky ground.

"Oh, Anya!" Mum came running to scoop her up, as she started to howl.

Toby was so surprised by the noise

Anya was making that he stopped barking. He didn't much like loud noises either – unless he was the one making them. He whimpered and pulled at his lead, trying to get away.

"Ruby, can you get the wipes out of my bag?" Mum asked, examining the graze down the side of Anya's face.

Ruby nodded. But Toby was pulling and tugging at the lead, and she couldn't unzip the bag and hold him at the same time. She looped Toby's lead over a nearby branch, so she could get at the bag properly. "Here they are."

Toby wriggled anxiously. He didn't like to see Anya upset, and he certainly didn't like the wailing. But once Mum had found a couple of sweets in her bag, Anya seemed to cheer up miraculously, and let her wipe the graze clean. After that, Toby stopped worrying about Anya quite so much, and started to investigate the branch that Ruby had fastened him to.

He didn't like it, Toby decided. He couldn't move more than half a metre either way without the lead pulling on his collar and hurting his neck. He couldn't go and sniff at that clump of bracken, which smelled as though a couple of other dogs had been there before. He *had* to check that out properly. And there was a really good, big stick just out of reach, which he would love to chew. It wasn't fair! He shook himself crossly, making the tags on his collar jingle.

"It's all right, Toby, hang on a minute..." Ruby murmured. But she didn't even look round at him – she was still fussing over Anya.

Toby shook himself again, and his lead slipped off the end of the branch and thudded to the ground beside him. He stared at it in surprise. He hadn't meant for that to happen.

If Anya hadn't started to howl again, because Mum had accidentally wiped her face too hard, Ruby would have noticed what had happened and grabbed him. But she was giving Anya a hug to cheer her up.

Toby eyed them thoughtfully. They were busy. But there was no point in coming out for a walk, and then just sitting on the path the whole time. He pattered away, sniffing happily at the bracken. He expected that Ruby would come and catch him up in a minute anyway. Another dog had definitely been past – perhaps the one he'd heard barking earlier? He would go and find it. He scampered along the path, nose down, following the scent, and leaving Ruby and Anya and Mum far behind.

"Is she going to be OK?" Ruby asked Mum worriedly. It looked like a nasty cut, and it was still bleeding, even after Mum had wiped it a couple of times.

"It'll be fine," Mum said. "We need to go home and wash it properly though."

"It hurts!" Anya wailed. "An' my fleece! My best fleece!" It was her pink one with the hearts on, and it was stained with mud all down the side.

"Mum can wash it. It'll be dry by tomorrow, won't it, Mum?" Ruby hugged her little sister gently. "Toby didn't mean to scare you by barking like that. He thought he heard another dog. Didn't you, Toby?"

Ruby turned round to look at him. But Toby had gone.

Chapter Four

The wood was full of birds calling, and squirrels racing up and down the branches. Toby was so little and so light-footed that on his own, without Mum and the girls, he hardly made any noise at all – only the quiet shushing of his lead, trailing behind him through the leaves. So he saw far more of the wildlife than he had before. A robin fluttered from tree to tree – almost as if it was leading him on – and Toby followed, fascinated.

The wood was old, and some of the trees were very large, with odd twisted roots that made little bridges and holes along the path. It was natural for such a small dog to try to wriggle through these rather than going round them, but unfortunately Toby forgot about his lead. He was hurrying after the robin when he was pulled back with a sudden, horrible jolt. He yelped and turned round, thinking that Ruby had caught up with him and grabbed the end of his lead. He looked up crossly. Why hadn't she called him, instead of grabbing him like that? But Ruby wasn't there.

Instead, his lead was caught on a sticking-out root – stuck fast, as he found out when he tried to pull it away like he had earlier. Toby wriggled, and whined, and whimpered, and pulled, but it was no good. The lead wasn't budging this time.

Toby sat down, panting wearily. This was just the same as before – he was stuck, when he wanted to explore. He tried pulling again, but the other way, squirming backwards to pull off his collar, instead of trying to free the lead.

As usual, Ruby had checked Toby's collar before they set out, to make sure there was enough space so it didn't rub him and hurt. But that also meant that if Toby didn't mind squashing his ears and wriggling very hard, it wasn't actually that difficult to get the collar off.

He burst out of it like a cork from a bottle, rolling over backwards and landing in a pile of leaves. He picked himself up, and sniffed curiously at his collar and lead. He didn't like to leave them, somehow. But he was sure Ruby would come along soon, and she could unhook the silly lead for him. He'd let her put it back on him if she'd come and run with him, instead of standing around and spoiling a good walk.

He trotted off through the undergrowth. He'd lost sight of the robin, but now there was an interesting grey-furred creature that was scampering through the branches above him. He wasn't sure what it was, but it bounced and sprang very temptingly, and he was hoping it might come a bit lower. He barked at it, but that made it go faster and climb higher, and he had to run flat out to keep up.

"Toby! Toby!" came a far-off cry. That was Ruby calling him. He stopped for a second, but the squirrel stopped too, looking down at him so cheekily that he couldn't bear to let it go. He'd try to find Ruby in a minute, once he'd caught it. He set off at a gallop again, and the squirrel leaped through the trees ahead of him.

He was chasing it so desperately that he almost ran into an old lady, standing in the middle of a clump of bracken holding a pair of binoculars.

"Ssshh!" the lady whispered crossly.

Toby pulled up short, staring at her in surprise. She'd been so quiet, he simply hadn't noticed she was there.

There was a beating of wings and a pair of birds fluttered away, squawking in fright. Toby watched them go, and barked again excitedly.

The old lady sighed. "You've scared them away, you silly dog." Then she seemed to realize for the first time that he was all alone. "Where's your owner, hmm?" She looked around, expecting someone to come chasing after him, but the woods were silent. "You haven't got a collar! Who do you belong to? They shouldn't be letting you race around here on your own, there's a road close by. Come here… Here, dog…"

She stretched out a hand to him, but Toby had heard the irritated tone in her voice after he scared the birds, and now he didn't trust her. He backed away nervously, and as she took a step forward to grab him, he raced off.

He hurried back through the bushes to the path, suddenly wishing that he was with Ruby. He'd find her, and then maybe they'd be able to catch the strange furry grey animal in the trees together. Toby scurried down the path, expecting at any moment to come to the big trees where he'd lost his lead, and then, a little way on, to find Mum and Anya and, most importantly, Ruby.

But as he went further and further along Toby realized that this might not be the path he wanted. He looked around, and suddenly the trees all seemed so much larger and darker, and different. He had no idea where he was, or where Ruby was. He was lost.

"But we can't just leave him!" Ruby stared at her mum in horror.

"Ruby, we have to go, I'm afraid. We've been searching for ages." Mum was holding Anya in her arms, who was crying miserably, the graze on her face still bleeding a little. "I need to get Anya home and clean up her face. It's filthy, and we've left it nearly an hour like this."

"If we go home now, we might never find Toby! Just five minutes more, please, Mum." Ruby looked around, desperately hoping Toby might spring out of the bracken suddenly, and everything would be all right again. But they had searched everywhere, calling and calling. Toby seemed to have totally disappeared.

"I've phoned your dad, and he's going to leave work early so you can both come straight back and look. I'm really sorry, sweetheart, but we have to get home." Mum set off down the path, carrying Anya.

Ruby stood in the middle of the path, looking uncertainly one way and the other. She couldn't bear the thought of leaving Toby. Maybe he'd been frightened by something, and was hiding. He might come out in just a minute, if they were quiet.

"Ruby, please!" Mum called, heading for the bridge over the stream.

Ruby trailed after her, trying not to cry. But by the time they reached the car, the tears were streaming down her face.

Toby pattered down another path, sniffing hopefully. He was sure he could smell Ruby, but the scent was all over the place. It was very confusing. It didn't help that he was so hungry. He wanted to be back at home with Ruby, eating his tea.

Just then, he heard the rushing sound of the stream, and he trotted forward, peering down the steep bank at the water. They had come over the stream, and that had been before Anya had fallen over, he remembered.

He sat down at the top of the bank. Should he cross over again or not? He whimpered miserably, wishing he had run back to Ruby when she called him. No. He wouldn't cross over again. Ruby would wait for him where he'd left her, he was sure. By those big trees, where Anya had fallen over. He only had to find them. He turned away from the stream, and nosed along, trying to find the path. But so many dogs had walked through the woods that he was quite distracted, and kept losing Ruby's scent.

It was starting to get dark, and the woods were gloomy, and full of strange noises, rustlings and odd bird calls. For the first time, Toby began to wonder what else might be in the woods, as well as that grey creature he'd chased. He wondered if there was anything bigger.

The late afternoon shadows meant that Toby didn't even notice when he pattered over the stream further along its course, where it ran under a fence in a huge metal pipe. Toby was small enough not to pay much attention to the fence, he simply went under it, and he didn't see the pipe buried in the bank. So he was surprised to find himself almost back at the road.

He came around a corner of the path and pulled up short, staring at the wider verge at the edge of the little lane that led into the woods. He knew this! He was sure of it, even though he hadn't crossed the stream again. This was just a little way along from where they had left their car. But the space they had parked in was empty.

They had gone without him!

Chapter Five

Toby sat down on the path, miserably. He'd been about to find Ruby, he was sure of it. But it looked like she'd left without him. He couldn't understand why she would go away and leave him. Didn't she want him back? Was she cross because he'd frightened Anya?

He whimpered, staring across the lane at the space where the car should have been. Then he whirled round, his tail tucked in, and a tiny growl beginning in his throat.

Behind him was a tall man who'd come jogging down the path, his big white trainers shining, even in the gathering dusk.

"Hey, it's all right. I almost trod on you, didn't I, poor little thing? Sorry, I didn't spot you there. I was just running, and not really looking." The man crouched down, panting, and stared at Toby, smiling. "You might just be the smallest dog I've ever seen."

Toby glared back at him suspiciously, remembering the lady who had told him off before.

The man held out a gentle hand, and Toby sniffed at it. The man smelled of another dog, which wasn't good, but apart from that, Toby felt as though he could trust him. And he didn't know what else to do.

"Who do you belong to? Hey? You're not a stray, you're too well-looked after. Lovely shiny coat, and you're not skinny, even if you are a tiny thing. Where's your collar? I bet you've slipped your lead, haven't you? Little devil. Someone's going to be really worried about you."

Toby backed away slightly as the man's hand went to his pocket, but all he did was pull out something in a crinkly wrapper and open it. He broke off a piece, and held it out to Toby.

"It's not really the best thing to give a dog, but a little bit won't do you any harm. You try it, pup. It's good. I like them anyway, when I've been out for a run. Energy bar, that's what it is."

The thing smelled sweet and sugary, and it was making Toby hungrier than ever. He darted forward and snapped it out of the man's hand, bolting it down in one gulp.

"Nice, isn't it? Want some more? I wonder who you belong to. You must have come here on a walk with your owners, there's no houses close by, and

you're too little to have come far."
The man looked around thoughtfully.
"So where are they, mmm? I wouldn't
leave you galloping about the place on
your own, and it's starting to get dark."

He stood up again and looked
around. "Hello! Anyone lost a dog?"

The shout echoed through the trees,
but no one answered. The only sound
now was a light pattering, as it began
to rain.

"We're going to get soaked." He
looked down at Toby, who was
shivering and pressing himself back
against the bushes. "Sorry, pup. Did I
scare you, shouting like that?"

He broke off another piece of the
cereal bar, and this time Toby nibbled it
out of his hand, and let the man stroke

his head and pet his ears. "Yes, you're a lovely little boy, aren't you?" He sighed. "What are we going to do with you, that's the question. There's no cars left, and I can't hear anyone else around. I can't just leave you here, all on your own. You don't look to me like you've got any road sense at all..."

He stretched out his hand again, and this time Toby sniffed it eagerly, hoping for more food. But the man picked him up instead, very gently, but firmly enough that Toby didn't feel as though he was going to be dropped. He snuggled against the man's warm hoodie, feeling a tiny bit better. Of course, the man wasn't the same as Ruby, but he was warm, and friendly, and the sugary stuff was very nice.

"Come on then. You'd better come home with me, while I ring up the dog shelter." The man tucked Toby in the crook of his arm, and set off down the lane.

Toby stared back at the trees, and the greenish gloomy darkness that was settling between them. He didn't like it here. But what if Ruby came back for him and he'd disappeared? He wriggled in the man's arms, and howled. He had to stay and wait for Ruby! Surely she was going to come back? And now he wouldn't be there for her!

"Ssshh, ssshh, I know. But I can't leave you here, pup. Don't worry. We'll find your owners, I promise." The man frowned. "Well, I hope so, anyway..."

On her way back to the woods with Dad, Ruby peered anxiously out of the car window. She'd read so many stories about dogs finding their way home that she half expected to see Toby trotting down the road towards them.

"Dad!" She pointed to the grass verge. "We parked here, and went up that path." She looked at her watch. It had been an hour since they'd left. She'd had to wait for Dad to get home, and then they'd driven all the way back. Toby had been missing for two whole hours now.

Her dad parked the car. "Come on then." He got out, and peered into the darkening wood. "Don't worry, Ruby. He's probably just hiding from the rain."

Ruby shivered. Somehow the wood looked much less welcoming than it had straight after school, when the autumn sun had been bright and friendly. But she straightened her shoulders, and marched determinedly up the footpath, calling for Toby. He had to be here somewhere.

"Can you remember where Anya fell?" Dad asked, rushing after her. "He might have had the sense to go back to where you left him."

"I think so. It wasn't far from here, just the other side of the stream." Ruby hurried on, crossing over the bridge, and looking anxiously from side to side, calling until her throat started to hurt.

"I can't understand why he isn't coming," she told her dad, stopping at the top of a little slope, and staring around them hopelessly. "I know he's naughty, but he usually comes if I call him in the garden. He knows I'll give him treats, and cuddle him. Why doesn't he want to come back to us now?" She leaned against her dad, trying hard not to cry. If she started, she knew it would be hard to stop.

"Ruby, don't worry. This place must be full of amazing smells for a dog..." Dad hugged her. "He's bound to be off chasing a squirrel or something. And remember what he was like when we met that German shepherd in the park. He might have chased off after another dog."

"We did hear another dog barking." Ruby nodded. "But it sounded a long

way away. Dad, he could be *anywhere*,"
she added. "What if he ran on to the
road?" she whispered.

Her dad sighed, and hugged her
tighter. "I don't think he'd do that, Ruby.
He's never tried it before, has he?"

"He's only been on a couple of
walks," Ruby pointed out miserably.
"And if he saw another dog he might."

Her dad shook his head. "There's no reason to think he went on to the road. He's probably sitting under a tree waiting for you. He'll be cross that you left him, knowing Toby!" Dad was trying to be cheerful, Ruby knew, but it wasn't really working.

She kept walking and calling, but still no Toby, or even an answering bark.

"Hey, what's that?" her dad asked, pointing at a flash of blue amongst a mass of twisted roots.

"His lead! That's Toby's lead!" Ruby's heart jumped wildly as she scrabbled for it, hoping that she might find Toby curled up fast asleep at the other end. He did sleep very deeply sometimes; he might not have heard them calling.

But all she found on the end of the lead was Toby's collar.

"Oh, Toby…" she whispered.

"He must have slipped it off," Dad said grimly. "Oh well, at least we know he was here. Come on, let's keep looking. We've got about another half-hour before it's completely dark."

Ruby swallowed as she looked around at the massive, hulking trees. There were holes and hiding places all over the wood, and it was getting darker by the minute, the light leaking away. She was scared, and she was with Dad.

And if she was scared, Ruby couldn't help thinking, as they hurried deeper into the trees, how frightened must Toby be, all alone?

Chapter Six

"I wish I knew what your name was," the man said to Toby, as he carried him down the lane and back towards the town. "I suppose I'm going to have to keep calling you pup. I'm Jake, by the way," he added, smiling down at Toby, who was curled into his elbow, watching everything they passed with anxious eyes. "And we're going back to my place, just for a bit, and then we'll take you to the shelter. Then hopefully your owners will come and find you..."

Toby glanced up at Jake's face, his ears flattening a little. There was a worried tone to the man's voice again, and he didn't like it.

"Yes, I know. No one would leave you behind on purpose, surely..." He sighed. "Anyway, we're nearly home. You're going to meet Mickey." He laughed. "Mickey's going to get a shock when he sees you. I only went out for a quick jog."

He searched in the pockets of his tracksuit trousers for the keys, as they came up to a little white-painted house. Toby leaned forward, listening intently. He could hear the clicking of claws on a hard floor, and a curious snuffling. There was another dog in there! It had to be the one that the man smelled of. He shifted a little nervously in Jake's arms. Usually he barked and barked at other dogs, but then he'd been with Ruby. Toby wanted everyone to know that she was his, and he was looking after her and Anya.

As the door swung open, a golden-brown head peered slowly round it, and stared suspiciously up at Toby.

"Hey, boy. I've brought a visitor. Don't panic, I don't think he's staying that long." Jake tucked Toby tightly under his arm, and crouched down to make a big fuss of his old golden retriever, murmuring a stream of reassuring words.

"It's lucky you're such a good boy, Mickey. You're not jealous. The pup's lost, poor little thing. We're going to help him get back home, that's all."

Mickey eyed Toby thoughtfully, as the dachshund puppy stared back. Then he wagged his long, feathery tail a couple of times, very slowly, and turned round, pacing back towards the kitchen and his cushion.

"You're going to have to be gentle with Mickey," Jake told Toby. "He's an old gentleman. Twelve years old, and he's a bit lame now. Don't go teasing him!" He put Toby down, watching carefully to see how he and Mickey were going to get along. Jake knew Mickey was really gentle, but he wasn't used to having other dogs in his house.

Toby looked around nervously, and then sidled after Jake as he headed into the kitchen, too.

"I know there's a leaflet from Oakley Shelter here somewhere. I was going to send them some money..." Jake muttered, searching through a pile of papers. "And now I'm sending them a sausage dog instead!" He pulled out a leaflet covered in photos of dogs.

"Ah, good. You two all right?" He looked down at Mickey, now curled up in his basket. Toby was sniffing thoroughly round the kitchen cupboards, and keeping his distance from the bigger dog. "OK. Let's call them." He tapped in the number, and then sighed. "I might've known. It's six o'clock already. No one's answering the phone." He put the phone back in its cradle slowly, and stared at Toby. "Now what do we do with you, pup? We'd better feed you, I suppose. That cereal bar won't keep you going for long."

He fetched a small bowl out of a cupboard, and put it down a little way from Mickey's big dog bowl, then poured food into both of them from a huge bag.

Toby flung himself at it as though he was starved, and gulped it down.

"Hopefully senior dog mixture won't do you any harm this once," Jake murmured, watching with a smile as Toby gobbled the dry food. "Let's get you some water as well."

Toby finished his food, and had a long drink of water. Then he watched Mickey, who was still slowly eating his bowlful. He edged a little closer, and Mickey turned round and gave him a very meaningful stare. *Don't come near my dinner.*

Toby wriggled backwards on his bottom, and then scuttled under the kitchen table until Mickey had finished and paced back to his bed for an after-dinner snooze.

"You need to be a bit careful, pup," Jake told him, stroking his head. "Mickey's a lot bigger than you, and this is his house."

But Toby was a naturally confident little dog, and he didn't really understand how small he was, either. He was starting to feel a bit more at home now, and he pranced up to Mickey, and eyed the bigger dog with his head on one side.

Mickey stared back, his muzzle resting on the edge of his cushion. He was a beautiful tawny golden colour, but his coat was turning silvery now, all around his mouth and eyes. He yawned, showing his very large teeth, and Toby took a step back again, looking a bit more respectful.

Even the teeth didn't stop him for long, though. Toby wasn't used to being ignored, and he didn't like it. He pattered right up to Mickey, and yapped sharply at him.

Mickey laid his ears back. The strange little dog was barking at him now, when he was trying to sleep.

Jake took a few steps closer. He trusted Mickey, but he wasn't taking any chances.

Toby wagged his tail excitedly and barked again, even louder, wanting to get a reaction out of the bigger dog.

Mickey looked over at Jake, his eyes wide, as if he was saying, *Rescue me from this thing!* But Jake only watched, smiling a little.

Toby crept closer, head down with his front paws flat against the kitchen floor, yapping and whining, his tail wagging. He was starting to enjoy this now. Maybe the big dog was scared of him!

Mickey huffed out a deep, irritable breath, and stood up, towering over the cheeky puppy. He put out a massive golden paw, and stood on one of Toby's too-long dachshund ears.

Toby wriggled and whined, but Mickey had him pinned. It was a clear message. *This is my house. You do as you're told.*

The puppy rolled over – as far as he could with Mickey holding his ear down – waving his paws in the air to show he gave in, and at last Mickey removed his paw. Toby stayed on his back, showing off his tummy apologetically, until Mickey sat down in his bed.

Finally, Toby turned over and wriggled forwards, creeping closer to the cushion as Mickey watched him. At the edge of the cushion, the puppy looked up hopefully, and the old dog nuzzled him. With a pleased little squeak, Toby hustled on to the cushion, and sat down next to Mickey. He did keep glancing up at the big dog, though, making sure he wasn't about to get the ear treatment again.

Jake laughed. "Taught him his place, have you, Mickey? Can he share your bed for tonight then?"

Mickey sighed, and slumped down on the cushion, squishing Toby up against the edge. But the puppy didn't seem to mind. He closed his eyes, and snuggled himself up to Mickey's broad back, so he was half lying on top of the bigger dog – and then the pair of them went to sleep.

"Where's Toby?" Anya asked, as Ruby pushed open the kitchen door, the lead dangling from her hand.

Her little sister was sitting at the table with their mum, eating a boiled egg and toast soldiers, her favourite tea. There was a big white gauze square over her grazed face, but she looked much more cheerful.

Ruby gulped, and then turned round and raced upstairs to her bedroom. She couldn't face explaining to Anya. And then she was going to have to tell Auntie Nell that they'd lost her precious puppy, as well!

She sat down on her floor, leaning against the warm radiator and sniffing. Toby liked to snuggle up here, too. He wasn't allowed to sleep in her room, but she carried him up to play sometimes.

Her bedroom door creaked open slowly, and Anya peered round it. "Are you cross?" she whispered.

Ruby shook her head. She hadn't thought to be cross with Anya – her little sister hadn't meant to fall over.

"Did Toby run away cos I fell over?" Anya said sadly.

Ruby put out her arms for Anya to come and hug her. "It wasn't your fault. I should have looked after him better."

"Oh, Ruby! You were helping me look after Anya." She hadn't seen her mum come in too. "It was just a horrible accident. I'm sure we'll find him. Dad can take you back to the woods really early in the morning."

Ruby nodded, but tears were sliding down her cheeks. "He'll be scared out there, Mum. It's so dark, and there's street lights here, there aren't any out there in the woods! And he'll be cold and hungry." She hugged Anya tighter, and her sister snuggled against her.

"We'll find him tomorrow, Ruby, I promise," Mum said.

Ruby nodded. But how could Mum promise that when no one knew where Toby was?

"Hey, pup!"

Toby yawned and opened his eyes. Why was Ruby waking him up, in the dark?

Then he sat up properly, looking around in panic. That wasn't Ruby!

"Sshh, don't worry. I just thought you might need a quick trip out to the garden before I go to bed. I'm not sure whether you're house-trained yet." Jake opened the back door, and the security light came on, sending an orangey light into the kitchen, and all of a sudden, Toby remembered where he was.

Or actually, where he *wasn't*. He wasn't at home in his lovely red basket with Ruby asleep upstairs. He was lost.

He whimpered, staring out at the strange, dark garden.

"I know. We'll find your owners tomorrow, hopefully. We'll ring the shelter again in the morning." Jake picked him up, and carried him out into the garden. "Go on, just a quick wee, then you can go back to sleep."

Toby wandered out on to the lawn, sniffing the night smell of wet grass. Everything was different, and wrong! Where was Ruby? Why hadn't he just stayed and waited for her? Then he would be home by now.

He sat down, raised his head to the sky, and howled.

Chapter Seven

"What if someone's found him and doesn't know who he belongs to?" Ruby said worriedly, looking back at Dad as they hurried into the woods early the next morning. It was chilly, and leaves were whirling on the cold wind.

"He's microchipped too, remember," Dad pointed out. "If someone takes him to a vet or the dog shelter, they'll be able to scan his microchip, and then they'll call us."

"So why haven't they?" Ruby wailed. "Maybe he got stuck down a badger hole! Auntie Nell said that ages and ages ago dachshunds were bred to chase badgers down their holes. Are there badgers in Norbury Copse, Dad?"

"Probably," Dad admitted. "But I don't think Toby would chase one…"

"He would!" Ruby told him sadly. "He tried to show that German shepherd who was boss, didn't he?"

"Excuse me…" someone behind them called breathlessly.

Ruby wheeled round in surprise. She'd been so busy imagining Toby stuck down a badger's sett, that she hadn't seen the old lady coming up the path after them. She hadn't expected anyone else to be here at half-past seven in the morning.

"Have you lost a dog? I'm sorry, I heard you calling…"

"Yes!" Dad replied, and Ruby raced up to the old lady.

"Have you seen my puppy?" she gasped. "Do you know where he is?"

"A little brown-and-black dachshund? I saw him yesterday – I come here birdwatching, you see. I did try to catch him, as I thought he might be lost, but he ran off again."

"That's Toby," Ruby whispered. "Did you see which way he went?" she added, rather hopelessly.

"No, but..." the old lady paused thoughtfully. "There was a man jogging, and I saw him again as I went back home. He had a little dog with him, and it might have been the same one..."

"A man's taken Toby!" Ruby gasped. "He's stolen him, he must have, or why didn't he call us?"

Dad hugged her. "Don't panic. Toby slipped his collar, remember? Perhaps the man took him to the police station. Or the dog shelter in town! That's more likely. We'll go home and call them. Thanks so much," he told the old lady. "You've been really helpful."

"I do hope you find him," the lady smiled. "He's a sweet little thing."

Ruby nodded. She was right – Toby was so little. Far too little to be out on his own. *He's at the shelter,* she told herself firmly. *He has to be...*

Dad put down the phone, making a face. "Answering machine. But the recorded message says Oakley Shelter opens at nine..."

He checked his watch. Ruby had been up at six wanting to go back to Norbury Copse, and it was still only half-past eight. "It'll take us twenty minutes or so to get there," he said thoughtfully.

"Let's go!" Ruby grabbed his hand and started pulling him towards the front door.

They sped off in the car, Ruby waving to Mum and Anya, who were watching from the door. Anya was really missing Toby, too. She'd been up almost as early as Ruby had, and when Ruby and Dad got back from the woods, Ruby had found her little sister sitting in Toby's basket, looking confused and sad.

As they drove through town to the shelter, Ruby leaned forward, her fists clenched so tightly her arms ached.

"Relax, Ruby," said Dad. "You're not making us go any faster. The shelter doesn't open for another quarter of an hour, anyway, and we're nearly there."

Ruby was out of the car the moment they stopped in the car park, and she was off, running towards the doors to the shelter. But it was still locked, and she rattled it uselessly.

"It's only five to," Dad called, following her across the car park.

Ruby paced up and down as they waited outside, checking her watch every ten seconds or so, certain each time that it must be nine o'clock by now.

At last, they saw a figure coming towards the glass doors, and a young woman smiled at them as she put the key in the lock.

Ruby hung on to Dad's arm, as the woman swung the door open. "Wow, you're keen!" she said cheerfuly. "Have you come to see about adopting a dog?"

Dad shook his head. "I'm afraid not. We're really hoping that our puppy is here. We lost him yesterday afternoon."

"Oh, right." The young woman looked doubtful. "I haven't heard about a puppy being brought in." She saw Ruby's face fall, and added quickly, "But I wasn't here yesterday, so don't take my word for it. I'll have to check with one of the others. Come on in, anyway."

She led them into the reception area. Ruby could hear the noise of barking from down the passage that led into the main shelter area. She strained her ears, trying to hear Toby's sharp dachshund bark. But it was too hard to pick it out. There was a clang of metal too, which she guessed was the food bowls being put out.

"There's nothing on the computer about a new puppy..." The woman was frowning as she tapped at the keyboard. "Let me go and ask Lucy. She's the manager, and she was in yesterday."

Ruby swallowed. It felt as though there was a huge lump stuck in her throat, and she was fighting back tears. "Dad, where can he be, if he's not here?" she whispered chokily.

"Don't get ahead of yourself," Dad murmured, hugging her. "He might be here." But he didn't sound all that hopeful.

A dark-haired woman came into the

reception area. "Hi, I'm Lucy Barnes. Bella says you're looking for a lost puppy? I'm really sorry, but we didn't have any dogs brought in yesterday."

"None at all..." Dad murmured worriedly.

"Where can he be, then?" Ruby asked, giving up the fight with the tears, and feeling them trickle down her cheeks.

"It may take a couple of days for him to get to us," Lucy explained gently. "Don't give up. Someone may have found him, and they could be holding on to him to see if they can find the owner themselves."

"That man might have stolen him," Ruby sobbed. "The old lady said she saw a man carrying a dog."

"Let me take your number, and the details of your puppy," Lucy suggested. "Then if someone brings him in to us, we'll get straight back to you."

"Thanks. He's a dachshund puppy, fifteen weeks old, and he's brown and black," Dad explained, and Lucy keyed the details into the computer.

"He's called Toby," Ruby gulped.

"And he went missing yesterday?"

"Yes, from Norbury Copse. He's microchipped – that should help, shouldn't it?" Dad asked hopefully.

Lucy smiled. "That's great. If he's brought in to the police, or a vet's, they'll call you straight away."

"Right. Well, thanks, Lucy. Come on, Ruby." Dad led her out to the car park. "I'm sorry, sweetie. Look, we'll call in at the police station on the way back. Maybe he got taken there. And if not, we'll pick up some rolls of sticky tape on the way home, then we can make a poster and put it up on all the lamp posts."

Ruby nodded, but tears started welling up in her eyes again. If they put up LOST posters, it meant they really had no idea where Toby was at all.

Chapter Eight

Ruby trailed across the car park, tears still trickling down her cheeks even though she kept wiping them away. Dad had his arm around her, but it wasn't making her feel any better.

Dad was just unlocking the car when Ruby heard someone calling behind them, and running footsteps.

"Wait a minute!" Lucy, the centre

manager, was chasing them across the car park, looking excited. She spoke into the phone in her hand, "Yes, I've caught them. A brown-and-black dachshund? That's wonderful!"

Ruby turned round to look at Lucy, her eyes wide with sudden hope. "Someone's found him!" she whispered.

Lucy nodded at her, smiling hugely as she listened to whoever it was on the other end of the phone.

Ruby felt like grabbing the phone. She wanted to know where Toby was – now now now!

Finally Lucy ended the call, and grinned at Ruby and Dad. "Thirty-six Elm Lane. A very nice-sounding man called Jake Harper went jogging in Norbury Copse last night, and found a little brown-and-black dachshund puppy, with no collar or lead. He rang us, but we'd closed, so he tried again just now to ask if it was OK to bring the puppy over." Her grin got even bigger. "I told him we'd save him the trouble and send you there instead! I hope you don't mind…"

"Thank you!" Ruby flung her arms round Lucy, and hugged her tight. "Oh, that's the best news!" She let go and looked up at Lucy worriedly. "It has to be Toby, hasn't it?" she asked. "There couldn't be another dachshund in the woods…"

"Jake was sure it was your puppy. The age sounded about right, and dachshunds aren't that common. Now go and get him!"

Dad smiled at Lucy. "Elm Lane, right? Thanks for all your help. Come on, Ruby!"

"Bye!" Ruby jumped into the car, fighting with her seat belt. She was suddenly so nervous that her fingers seemed to have stopped working. It had to be Toby, it just had to. She couldn't bear to be disappointed again.

Toby was lying in the middle of the cushion, with his head on his paws, watching as Mickey ate his breakfast.

It was dog food from a tin this time – different to the biscuits Toby had at home. He quite liked the smell, but somehow he wasn't very hungry, even though there was also a big helping for him.

"You're quiet this morning." Jake crouched down by the basket. "I hope you're not sickening for something. Especially as I think I've found your owner. A young lady's very worried about you, apparently. Maybe you're just missing her, mmm?" He stood up. "Well, it won't hurt you to miss one breakfast, I suppose, if you don't feel like it. Do you want to go out? Quick sniff round the garden? No?" He patted Toby's smooth head. "Not long now, pup. Cheer up."

Toby had lifted his head to look at Jake while he was talking, but now the big man was walking away, he let it flop back down. He didn't want food, and he didn't want to go out in the garden. He wanted Ruby.

He wanted Ruby pouring out his dog biscuits, and watching him lovingly while he wolfed them down. He wanted to race up and down the garden with her and Anya. He liked Jake, and Mickey was good to share a bed with for one night. But he didn't want to stay here. He'd never really known another dog before. Especially not one that stood on his ears! This was Mickey's house, and Jake was Mickey's special person. Mickey had made that very plain, and Toby didn't mind. He just wanted to be back home with Ruby.

Elm Lane wasn't far from the shelter, and Ruby and her dad pulled up outside number thirty-six about ten minutes later.

They could hear barking from inside, even before they rang the bell, and Ruby looked up at Dad with shining eyes. It was a squeaky sort of bark. A bossy little dog's bark…

"It's him, isn't it?" Ruby whispered, and Dad nodded, beaming.

On the other side of the door, Toby scrabbled and yelped, clawing at the wood panels. He could hear Ruby! She'd come to find him!

As the door opened, a small brown-and-black ball of fur hurled itself at Ruby, barking and yapping.

She picked him up, laughing and crying at the same time. "Toby! Where did you go? We looked everywhere for you! Oh, I missed you!"

Toby licked her face lovingly, then went back to jumping and wriggling, and wagging his tail so hard his whole back end wagged too. He leaned dangerously far out of Ruby's arms to lick Dad too, and even licked Jake.

Jake laughed. "Yes, you're happy now, aren't you, pup?"

"Thank you for finding him," Ruby said shyly, so quietly that Jake could hardly hear her over the mad barking.

"That's all right. He didn't have a collar. I suppose he must have lost it."

"He was wearing one." Ruby nodded. "My little sister fell over, you see, and I was helping Mum cheer her up. I hooked Toby's lead over a branch, and by the time we'd sorted Anya out, he was just gone!" Her voice squeaked with fright as she remembered it. "I bet you went off chasing squirrels, didn't you?" she asked Toby. "The woods were full of them."

Then her eyes widened, as Mickey lumbered into the hallway to see what was going on. "Oh! You've got a dog, too." She looked worriedly up at Dad, and then at Jake. "I'm really sorry if Toby fought with him…"

Jake laughed. "Actually, he tried being a bit bossy, but Mickey stood on him. After that he was very good!"

"Stood on him?" Ruby gasped, looking at Mickey. He was huge.

He looked like he could squash Toby.

"Just on one ear, just for a moment. His way of showing Toby who was in charge, I think. Has he been difficult with other dogs before, then?"

Ruby shuddered. "He barks at them. It's like he thinks he's as big as they are." She looked down at Toby, who'd wriggled out of her arms and was dancing round Mickey's legs, nuzzling him playfully. "But he's being so nice with your dog now!"

Jake grinned. "Maybe he just needed a lesson on who's in charge of the pack. Have you tried puppy parties?"

Dad shook his head. "I've not even heard of them. Is it like training? We're booked in for a class that starts in a couple of weeks."

"Oh well, the people running your training might do puppy parties too – you should ask. It's like a safe place for young dogs to get to know each other. It teaches them how to get along, and work out who's in charge. But you're there to step in if there's any problems."

"You know lots about dogs," Ruby said wistfully. She wished she knew as much. She felt like she'd let Toby down so badly, losing him in the woods, even if Mum had said it wasn't her fault.

Jake smiled at her. "He really missed you, you know. Mickey distracted him last night, but when I woke him up to go out for a wee before I went to bed, he seemed miserable. And this morning, he just sat in the basket looking lonely – didn't even want any breakfast. He didn't want me, even if I have been a dog-owner for years. He's your puppy."

Ruby nodded, watching as Toby wove in and out of Mickey's legs. Then he stopped suddenly, looking round, as if he was checking that Ruby was still there.

She crouched down, and he raced over to lick her hand quickly, before going back to his game.

"See?" Jake nodded at Ruby. "Your dog."

Ruby smiled. It was true. And she was going to make sure she never lost him again.

Dad had called home to let Mum and Anya know that they'd found Toby, so Ruby wasn't that surprised to find Anya in the front garden waiting for them. She was standing on the bottom of the gate, peering over the top, and she waved madly as soon as she saw the car.

For once, Dad had let Ruby carry Toby on her lap instead of putting him in his travel crate. Every so often, as they drove along, he turned and looked up at her, as though to check she was still there, and he kept giving her hands loving little licks.

"Toby, Toby!" Anya flung open the gate, and rushed over to them, with Mum chasing after her.

"Oh, Ruby, I'm so glad you've got him back," Mum said, smiling through the car window.

Ruby got out of the car, and Toby licked Anya, very gently. He could see that the white patch on her face meant he had to be careful.

"Good boy," Ruby whispered. She went in through the gate, expecting Toby to jump down and race around the garden, like he usually did. But this time he stayed snuggled in Ruby's arms.

There was nowhere else he would rather be.

Coming soon:

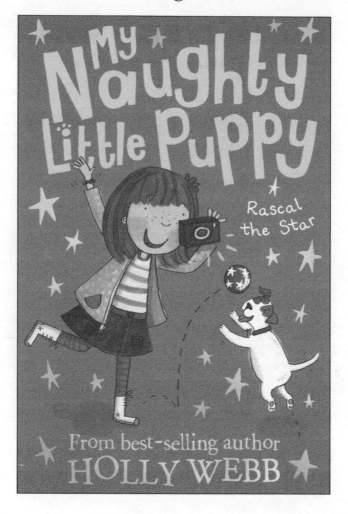

My Naughty Little Puppy

Rascal the Star

From best-selling author HOLLY WEBB